Scratching the Surface

Quick Fiction
100 Stories in 100 words or less

MERCEDES DOUGLAS

Scratching the Surface

MERCEDES DOUGLAS

WALTHAM PARK CREATIVE GROUP

DEDICATION

This book is dedicated to my mother, Hortense McCarthy (1943 -1977), who has been a great inspiration in my life. She was a wonderful woman that I had the pleasure of knowing for eleven precious years. In the summer of '77, a few months before my mom passed away, our family went on vacation, back home to Jamaica. While on our trip we stopped in a bookstore and my mom bought me the last book I'd ever receive from her and the first book to change my life to become a writer. The book is Little Women, by Louisa May Alcott and I still have it. Now, years later I am able to write my own stories to share with others.

Thanks Mom.

Table of Contents

INTRODUCTION

In the winter of 2011, I started a blog, Casually Speaking, on the Wordpress platform as a way to share my ideas and thoughts. As I began to post information on the blog one of the things I thought was missing were fictional short stories, which I love to write. I knew the stories had to be really short, to keep the reader's attention. They would also need to be straightforward but with impact, and that's how the challenge of writing a complete story in one hundred words or less came about. After writing the first few stories I got the idea to write a few more and put them in a book. That idea lingered in my mind, but I didn't take action right away. I continued writing, basically as an exercise to sharpen my skills. It took four years for the idea to develop into a project and the project then turned into this book. Each story speaks volumes on life in general, through the experiences of the characters. The stories may remind you of a loved one; a good friend; somewhere you've visited or even of yourself. Escape into their world, for just a moment, and follow their journey. In no time you'll move from one story to the next and before you know it, you're done reading. I hope you find **Scratching the Surface** heart-warming and entertaining.

Mercedes

TRYING HARDER

"If at first…" you've heard it said, but those are just words
inside your head.

You're tired of trying and seeing things fail. You question
your future and if hope will prevail.

Don't worry about the how and why. You owe it to
yourself to give it a try.

Then, deep within your courage comes through. Flaming
the spark to start anew.

One step, two steps, three steps, four. There ya go! You got it.
Just try a little bit more.

Now, you're finished and made it to the end. I knew all

along you could do it my friend.

COOKING IN THE KITCHEN

My wife, Jeanie has gotten friskier over the years and sometimes I have to run away from her. I'm not the young man I used to be; I'll be eighty-two this spring, but I try to keep up with her. A couple of years ago our neighbor down the street told Jeanie about how she spiced up her marriage. No sooner did my wife go out and buy a bunch of rosemary plants to put in the garden. Since then, I never know when Jeanie is gonna turn the corner anywhere in the house with hunger in her eyes.

MAKE IT WORK

Sometimes you gotta know when your relationship isn't working out. You can tell. The communication becomes distant. What used to make you laugh now ticks you off. Spending time apart is sometimes better than when you're together. At least that's what I heard my boyfriend say on the phone. But I've invested over seven years with this man; I'm not gonna let it fade away like that. I know I can make it work; it can't end like this. I just need to remind him I'm the best thing that's happened to him. Who wouldn't want to be with me?

GIMME A BEAT

My heaviest weight was three hundred pounds, three years ago, when my doctor diagnosed me with high blood pressure and pre-diabetes. My weight didn't bother me before I went to the doctor, but it started to get in the way of my health. I was home one night and had the radio on and found myself tapping my feet, before I knew it I was dancing. I loved it so much I kept dancing. These days I'm lighter on my feet and I even found a dance partner; she actually fell for this big-hearted guy who likes to two-step.

CHANGE OF PLANS

Devin was dressed in his military uniform and looked sharp. As Tanya walked through the doors of the church there wasn't an empty seat. She trembled as she walked down the aisle, her father held her by the arm until they got to the front. She stood there wearing her wedding dress and didn't care what people would say, she wanted to always remember the details of the day. Tanya looked down at Devin then tears swelled up in her eyes. He was killed in action serving his country. What should have been their wedding day, respectfully, was Devin's funeral.

DOUBLING UP

Through the back door Jake ran out, right behind him was Paula, his classmate. Paula thought Jake was the cutest boy she ever saw; however, Jake didn't feel the same way, he preferred playing with frogs. Paula was fast and caught up to Jake by the oak tree. She grabbed the tail of his shirt and dragged him down to the ground. Paula looked around to hear hysterical laughter and saw a boy standing at the back door. Jake explained to Paula he had a twin brother, Jack. Through the front door, Jack ran out, with Paula right behind him.

GREAT CATCH

My lady is the best thing that has happened to me; she's only brought me good luck. I'll never forget the day I first laid eyes on her, ooh, what a sight! It was summer when I strolled down by the San Francisco bay and saw her in all her beauty. Somehow, I just knew she was the one for me. In the beginning I spent a lot of money to make sure she looked her best. It's been a few years and I know she was a good investment, because I'm constantly complimented on how great my boat looks.

ROTATING BIRTHDAY

My Aunt Flora will be 78 on her next birthday, but she can't stand it, not getting older, but the date. She was born on December 30th and she's longed believed that it's the worst birthday to have. Aunt Flora says that by her birthday people have spent most of their money on presents for family and friends to celebrate Christmas, Hanukkah or Kwanzaa, and have just enough left to celebrate New Years. So, she decided many years ago to acknowledge December 30th, but she celebrates her birthday on July 4th, while everyone in America is celebrating too.

LEADING THE FLOCK

When Oliver Sheppard first accepted his job, he was filled with excitement and trepidation. He was young and eager to make a meaningful impression into the lives of the people that he would be in contact with. Oliver spent many years preparing his craft and seeking ways he could improve, but little did he know his occupation would be accompanied by a serious work hazard. This good-looking preacher pastoring his first church suddenly found his counseling sessions completely booked by a host of single women seeking his attention.

BLOWING IN THE WIND

All the air inside of Chloe left her body and she knew it was over; she was dead. She didn't feel a thing. No more pain. No more chemo. It was cloudy around her and then she saw a light in the distance. Her family was at the cemetery, as Chloe watched her mother appearing strong but knowing her heart was breaking. Chloe wanted to send a message to her but didn't know how. She waved her hand, then suddenly on a peaceful spring afternoon came a fierce and powerful gusty wind, then it stopped. Chloe gave her last goodbye.

THE CHECKLIST

Kaye (16 yrs. old): *My man will be tall, dark and gorgeous. He'll be polished and well educated. He must be ambitious and make enough money to take care of our four kids and me then we'll live happily ever after.*

Kaye (34 yrs. old): *My husband is short, 5'7", with an average build and so handsome. He can be rough around the edges but he's sharp and smart. Our business is thriving and we support each other. We couldn't have children, but we adopted two boys. We're happy and we take each day at a time.*

ROCK ON

My 72 year old abuela* plays in a rock and roll band, Los Mujeres del Fuego* and I don't know about anyone else, but I'm her biggest fan. She's the drummer in the group and has been playing with her friends for about six years now. The group gets regular gigs all over the city and has even played the Governor's Ball. My abuela had to change her lifestyle a few months back, because of her bypass surgery. Nowadays, she says she'd rather rock out tunes than sit around in a rocking chair. "La vida es corta, Roca en!" *

* *Abuela* = *grandmother*
* *Los Mujeres del Fuego* = *women of fire*
* *La vida es cora, Roca en!* = *Life is short, Rock on!*

INTO THE DARKNESS

Evil stumbled in the darkness, trying to break my peace. I noticed it at a distance as it attempted to blend into my daily routine. I shouldn't have been shocked it showed up, because it was only a matter of time, things were going too well. I remembered what to do and stood my ground and stayed strong because I knew evil couldn't hang around forever. Before I knew it, evil sauntered pass me as I held my breath. Then, I exhaled. I can only guess when evil would pay another visit.

SWIMMING LESSONS

When my Grandpop first taught me how to swim he'd say, "Don't be afraid of the water." He sat at the end of the dock and encouraged me to stay in the water longer than I really wanted to. "You're in the belly of the earth, young man! Feel the movement and relax your body." I was thrilled when Grandpop would get in the water and swim, leaving his wheelchair back at the dock. My Grandpop taught me not to be fearful but remain calm, regardless of the situation and find strength from inside to keep moving.

TIMING IS EVERYTHING

Wake up and get ready, perform your usual routine, then make your way through to work. Clock in, right on time.

—Time is ticking

Years of training to perfect your skills. Pursuing interests that align with your passion.

—Time is ticking

Discovering the joy in your contribution to the earth and realizing your efforts were not in vain.

—Time is ticking

You've done the best job that you knew how to do. There's nothing more that can be done.

—Time is up.

Clock out.

SPECIAL EVENING

I saw her through the crowd, looking beautiful in her little black dress. She changed a bit. Her hair is longer, but I would recognize her anywhere. She still had a sweet angelic smile; I hope she never loses that. Would she remember me? Would she want to spend time with me? I didn't travel all this way, just to get a glimpse, so let me… oh, she saw me and here she comes running towards me. I grab her in my arms and squeeze her tiny waist. "Daddy, I'm glad you made it to my recital!"

HIGH MAINTENANCE

Time caught up with me after I've been trying to run away from it for years. After my thirty-ninth birthday and the birth of my fourth child, I noticed what was firm was now soft and gravity was working against me. I needed some help. I wasn't ready to face all those bodily changes, although I know I should have. I decided to do something to whip my body in shape, so I swam and played racquetball. Funny, those were just minor concerns because as long as I'm still here, living strong, I'll be a survivor of breast cancer.

XIOMARA DANCING

Xiomara Vasquez, born in Panama, was a dancer with a wandering heart. Xiomara moved to her own rhythm, she heard fast beats when others moved slowly. At 22, she traveled to Brazil and stepped in time to the sounds of Rio de Janeiro. Her heart found joy and was free to fly as high as her dreams would take her. On stage Xiomara heard her name in a distance being called from the crowd; it encouraged her to keep dancing. Then the music stopped, Xiomara opened her eyes and stretched out her hand to receive her college diploma.

HANG ON

Hanging on the edge of hope, with nothing to lose, Jackson packed her things, with her infant son in tow. New York was a far cry from Sarasota, Florida, but as an artist there was nowhere else for Jackson to grow. She was commissioned to paint a series of paintings for an art curator who came across her portfolio online. Jackson would receive a stipend for living expenses, half her pay up front and the remainder upon completion. To think just a month ago, Jackson had $100 in the bank; her boyfriend dumped her and she lost her waitressing job.

FULL DISCLOSURE

My senior year in college, I realized I wasn't gonna have
enough money for medical school unless I took a hefty loan,
which I didn't want. A friend tried to help and told me about
a job at the club, Luscious Lips, where as a stripper I'd only
work a few hours and make lots of money. I got a job there
as a bartender instead. I found a way to entertain customers,
while serving drinks and kept my clothes on. Next year, is
my last year in medical school and I'll be proud to leave with
no debt.

HOME TRAINING

My father was hated by our family for the horrible things he did to my little sister and me. My mother stood by and allowed him to harm us. She didn't protect us; then again she needed protection from him herself. My mother left my father and my sister went off to college. A few years ago, my hate turned to pity after he was diagnosed with Multiple Sclerosis and confined to a wheelchair. I still live at home and take care of my father, not because I want to, but only because real men take care of their family.

ANTI-AGING

People have been fascinated by Paulette's youthful appearance for years. She is in her seventies, retired, widowed, living on her own, with three adult children who blessed her with ten grandchildren, but the woman doesn't look older than fifty. What makes her look so young; beauty creams, the food she eats or dare I say plastic surgery? Finally, Paulette was ready to talk about her secret for anti-aging. She said it was simple, she likes to party…because everyday is a gift so she always finds different ways to celebrate life.

RULES OF THE HOUSE

As one of nine children, it wasn't easy having peace in our home, but my parents laid out the house rules and it helped to keep things in order.

- Family first
- No fighting/arguing, words have power use them wisely.
- No stealing, value yourself.
- No lying, the truth isn't hard to find.
- Be kind to others, it's the human thing to do.
- Be smart about your choices, you have to live with them afterwards.
- Love yourself first and find the best you from inside.

As an adult, I use these rules in my home and they work for my family too.

FIRST STEPS

Toby took his first steps today, we are so proud of him. He's been trying hard for some time, but he would often fall down in frustration. Toby wants to be independent, he won't hold on to his Dad or me; he has a determined personality. At night, when he settles in and I get him ready for bed, I always remind him how much we love him and encourage him to do his best. No matter what, we're behind him. Today, Toby took his first steps, one year, four months and six days after his accident playing college football.

EQUAL SHARE

The cancer had spread and time was running out for Mitchell. He already had a will but it didn't include the twelve million he hid away. Mitchell knew he wanted his four children to split the money he worked hard for; they would have access to the money a year after his death. Early in his career, the company he worked for took as much as they could from him, vacations, family time and weekends. Gradually he decided to take a little back for himself. At the funeral, his co-workers said he was the best accountant the company ever had.

JAIL HOUSE ROCK

Jesus came to visit me while I sat in the parking lot of the county jail, struggling with my conscience for more than an hour. I just know it was Him. I drove nearly fifty miles to visit my father who was locked up for a multitude of charges. Jesus sat beside me and reminded me about forgiveness. I cried. I felt a hand on my shoulder; when I looked around there was no one there. I went inside the jail to see my father. We spoke for a while and when I left the jail I felt free.

TRAVELING

Houston, Texas told me I had to be large and in control, so I moved on.

Las Vegas, Nevada told me to take a chance regardless of the stakes, I won't forget that, but I moved on.

Portland, Oregon told me not to be afraid, to speak up for myself, which was fabulous, but I moved on.

Chicago, Illinois told me to get a grip and hold on tight to the joy. Guess what, I moved on.

I took all my lessons with me to a cool and comfortable south island and now I'm learning how to relax.

SOMETHING OF HIS OWN

"I take what's mine," José said.

"You're telling me, you own that BMW?" Officer O'Connor asked.

"I couldn't own a car like that? Why, because I'm seventeen; because I'm Hispanic? José questioned.

"Listen kid, I don't see that you have any priors, but the arresting officer stated your paperwork doesn't show you own that car!" Officer O'Connor leaned in.

"That officer took one look at me, then my ride and made his judgment." José looked away.

A gentleman approached Officer O'Connor, "Excuse me? I see you're questioning my son, I'm Joseph Salazar, I own the car dealership on Fifth Street."

LOST AND FOUND

Being the wife of a Midwest preacher and the mother of six young children, at thirty-five, Madlin felt her life was slipping away from her; she wanted to find her life again. Madlin decided to share her story, first with a small women's group at the church, then she spoke at the local library. The crowd was interested in what she had to say. She gave several radio interviews and started speaking across the country. Her family has been supportive and has realized how vital Madlin has been in their lives after she began to share her life with others.

MY BOYFRIEND

Mama is in love with Rodrigo, my boyfriend. Oh, she's denied it many times, but I've seen how she looks at him and what she wears whenever he's around. We've been dating for nearly a year and Mama's been acting strange the past six months. I still live at home, so it's hard when Rodrigo picks me up for a date and Mama is drooling all over him; waiting on him hand and foot. She says she's just offering him southern hospitality. I wonder if she'll show Daddy the same treatment when he's back from his tour of duty.

SERVING TIME

Life was hard for Ellis Whitlock, the district attorney's son, for years he's tried to get his dad to spend more time with him. No matter what he did on the street he was careful to stay out of trouble because of who his father was, but trouble knew his address and visited him often. Then one-day trouble knocked hard on his door; this time not even his father could help him. Ellis went to court and got a sentence of ten to twelve years. Maybe now his dad will spend time with him, if he visits him in prison.

TEMPORARY HOUSING

Our space isn't that big, but it's enough for the three of us. The baby was in the hospital for months. It was really scary then… we thought we were gonna lose her, but she's better now. My wife and I didn't have enough insurance to cover the mounting hospital costs. We had to sell the house, it was painful but we didn't see any other way, and would you believe we still owe a few thousand more to the hospital. The most important thing is we're all together and we know living in our van is just temporary.

WORKING RELATIONSHIP

If I don't have you what will I do? You are why I look forward to waking up in the mornings and when I'm near you there's no better feeling. We've been together for a long time and developed a kind of rhythm that works. You keep me busy and maybe I don't get to hang out with friends or share special occasions with my family, I miss that, but you're the biggest part of my life. I can't let you go. I'll be with you for as long as I can because my job is my life.

LET ME ENTERTAIN YOU

He isn't that handsome, but he has lots of money and enjoys spending it on me. He said he wanted companionship, nothing sexual, and that was simple enough. We went out to eat; concerts, the theatre and sometimes we went to church. He told me I had a great spirit and a wonderful laugh. It's been two years since we've been socializing together and his wife doesn't seem to mind. I've seen her once or twice and she told me that keeping her husband entertained has done wonders for their marriage. I wonder if my husband would be as understanding?

SPEED DATING

I asked him:

" What do you do for a living?"

"Do you have kids?"

"Do you want a family?"

" What's your favorite movie?"

" Read any good books lately?"

" You don't read?"

" What's your job, again?"

" How long was your last relationship?"

"Before that?"

"And, before that?"

"Do I want to have dinner after this?"

" I'm not that desper… umm, hungry. "

I asked myself:

'How much longer do we have here?'

'I wonder if I can still catch a movie?'

'How did I talk myself into coming here, anyway?'

'Okay. Good. Time's up!'

DISTANT MESSAGE

"Hi, honey. I'm sorry I missed you; I guess you already left to pick me up from the airport. I know I tell you often how much I love you. You can't imagine. I'll love you always; don't forget that. The plane has..."

On September 11th, 2001, Flight 93 went down in a field, killing all on board, but not before several passengers were able to overtake the terrorists who hijacked the plane.

This message is a reminder of how precious love is because everyday she's glad she was late getting to the airport and missed that flight.

LATE NIGHT MEETING

He left the lights on in the kitchen with dinner covered on the stove. She'd been working double shifts at the hospital the past few months, getting home at midnight nearly every night, tired and drained from the day. He rolled out of bed and rubbed his eyes. From behind, he gently put his arm around her waist, slowly turned her to him and kissed her on the neck, her cheek and then her lips, "I'll start your shower," he said. "That's just what I need," she replied. "I got the job," he smiled, "now you can relax."

PEGGY'S CHECK BOOK

Peggy cared for her mother the last three years before her mom died of Alzheimer's. After paying the medical bills and funeral costs from the insurance money, Peggy still had lots of money leftover, which was what attracted Donovan to her initially. He quit his job and moved in with Peggy, but it was short lived. Peggy sold the house and decided to start fresh leaving the past behind, including Donovan. She was going to take control of her money and her life. Peggy climbed in the front seat of her Lincoln and smiled looking back in the rearview mirror.

TAKING NOTHING FOR GRANTED

For more than two decades the artists worked in the basement of the Washington, D.C. Historical Society, recreating works of art. The faithful six were skilled at their trade. They could take one glimpse of a famous painting, commit it to memory and reproduce the exact painting, right down to the detailed brushstrokes. Through the years the steadiness of their hands didn't produce the work, as quickly as before, at least that's what they told everyone. All six men retired the same year, gave up all their belongings and now live in their luxurious homes in the South of France.

SHARING THE WEALTH

In the village of Ooknatabe, the people have lived like royalty for generations. Each year, when the moon appeared to sit on the mountain's peak, heavy rains would fall and continue for weeks and weeks. When the rain finally stopped, the elders would kneel on the ground and pray; then they dug into the mud and gave thanks. As they pulled their hands out of the mud, gold coins would fall through their fingers in abundance. They'd share coins with nearby villages and keep what was left. And so, the village of Ooknatabe remains the richest village in the land.

SING-A-SONG

Monique Chavelle was in a hotel lounge in Paris sipping a vodka martini; her set was in fifteen minutes and she needed to calm her nerves. Monique longed to be back on the main stage with sold out concerts like she had ten years ago at the height of her career. She found ways to cope with her success and as a result she went from a sweet soprano to an average alto. At fifty-seven she still has a song in her heart and no matter the crowd, twenty or twenty thousand, there's nothing else she'd rather do than sing.

IS IT STILL RAINING?

It's been raining for a long time now. I just got home...
soaking wet... then settled in. There they are on the table,
the bills that have sat there for weeks. Instead of decreasing,
the pile keeps growing. It's raining harder. How am I gonna
catch up? When am I gonna get a break? I know tears aren't
gonna help me, so I'll just wipe them away. I can either
continue to ignore the bills or start with the ones that have
fallen on the floor and deal with them. Hmph looks like the
rain is starting to let up.

HARD WORKING

I had a plan. I would retire in the prime of my life and finally get a chance to enjoy a good round of golf. However, our company was bought out and the mid-level executives, like me, got a severance package. The company's stock plummeted and sadly there wasn't much of the pension left after all was said and done. **This wasn't part of my plan**. I've tried to get placed in a company to match my skills, between working two part-time jobs. I'm nearly sixty-seven and have to keep working, no time for retirement. **What's the plan now?**

LAST SUPPER

She asked for a steak, well done, mashed potatoes, asparagus and red velvet cake. She savored every bite and took her time eating, then wiped her mouth with a linen napkin. She thought the food was like home cooking and reflected on the last time she was home. What started out as a loving and peaceful evening ended with tempers flared and a regrettable action that would tear the family apart. Later that evening, she met with a priest and he read her last rites as they walked down the corridor to the chamber at the end of the hall.

WISHING YOU WELL

Everyone can use a little help every now and again, and in a neighborhood in Brooklyn that's what the community does. Behind the old Methodist church was a wishing well, it had been dried up for years, but it still had its bucket. One day one of the residents, who was going through a rough time, wrote a note asking for help and dropped the note in the bucket. A couple of people found the note and decided to help anonymously. Word got out about what happened and as people dropped in their notes others would pitch in to help.

GARDENING TIPS

What I learned in life my grandmamma taught me from gardening. She has breathtaking flower gardens but it takes hard work and *ya gotta* get down and dirty. Grandmamma picks plants to go in the best positions, whether they'd need more sun or have to be tucked in the shade. Some plants were meant to handle frigid temperatures while others can tolerate the heat. Grandmamma knows which plants will stick around for years and which ones will only last a season. She'd say, " people are like plants, choose the right ones to make your world beautiful."

EYES SHUT

I know it's coming and I'm not afraid. I close my eyes for a moment and try to remember as much as I can, then I smile. I look through the window and I'm still amazed at God's creations; the blue sky and the sun shining so brightly. Listening to the melody of birds as they sing. I'll miss it, but I can take the memories with me as I go…. it comforts me and let's me know I'm safe. Now I can rest because I have peace. I close my eyes.

SPARKLING

The women had planned for their European vacation for months; four friends, Maxine, Olivia, Ronnie and Inez, all thirsty for adventure. For two weeks they enjoyed the sites, great food and beautiful weather. The day before their flight home they came across a red pouch on the side of a cobblestoned road in Italy. Ronnie and Maxine were hesitant but Olivia and Inez grabbed the pouch and found diamonds inside. That night they tirelessly worked their crafting skills to create works of art. They all walked through the airport's customs section with elaborately decorated accessories: bracelets, headbands and diamond-studded sandals.

YARDIE

De boss a get pon mi nurves agen. Mi know seh me werk 'ard fah dis ya job, ann mi mek good good muny; but nuh mine wha mi do, de boss allways want moor from mi. Suh one dey mi stop ann ask 'im whapen. Listen wat 'im seh, "You are one of our best employees. You're dependable and dedicated to the job." Mi scratch mi 'ead ann den 'im seh, "I admire how Jamaicans are so hardworking and ambitious, I can relate. Is 'ow yuh tink me becum de boss? Yuh neva know seh I was Jamaican too?"

CRUSHING

You ever been in a pickle where you couldn't see your way out to save your life? Well, I guess lying in a stranger's bed, with that same stranger naked, sprawled across you and not breathing would be considered a jar full of pickles. He's twice my size and it was getting hard to breath. Last night, at the party he seemed nice, harmless really. I can see my mobile phone on the floor near the dresser and if I could wiggle from under him I'd break free. What was that? He's alive? He's alive! Oh, must be sleep apnea.

POSITIONING

Daddy used to say that women folk need to know their place, which was right behind a man. Only men worked in his office; the few women that did work there did the cleaning. Daddy was stubborn and thought any advice from women was for his personal entertainment. One day Daddy took ill and asked my sister, Mabeline and me to help out with the business. Much to his surprise we not only kept the business afloat but also helped it grow. Now, he sees a new place for women in business, anywhere they want to be.

CHECKMATE

You're not so big and bad. You're not as tough as you think. YOU are the biggest coward I know, hiding behind your mask. At first you fooled me into believing I was doing something wrong, that I made so many mistakes, but it was you all along. Yes, I admit when I'm wrong and own it, just like you should, but instead you use your words to make me feel like a failure. I became more aware of myself and began to understand my purpose. Decide your next move because as of now, I'm not playing your games anymore.

MOVING ON

They said I shouldn't pack up my family and move up north from Alabama, 'cause we might not be welcomed there. They said we wouldn't get farther than the county line 'cause the police would probably stop us. They said, "It's the 50's and a colored man can only find work as a janitor." Our family has been successfully living in Connecticut, while owning our own business, for over forty years now. They said a lot of things, but we paid them no never mind. We listened to our hearts and not the voices we left behind.

GIBSON MARKETING TOOL

For years, Gibson's Mechanic Shop has been a staple on the corner of Schenectady Avenue, but lately business has slowed down. Mr. Gibson quickly realized that he needed a clever marketing plan to drum up new business. After a few short weeks, while utilizing his new marketing tool, business picked up speed, so much so that the majority of his workload was fixing flats. Mr. Gibson didn't want his businesses to suffer because he runs the mechanic shop and also Gibson's Hardware next door. The hardware store has been doing well and recently increased its inventory of nails.

FATHERLY ADVICE

Father O'Malley cared deeply for the parishioners and the struggles they had in their lives. Of all the clergy at Saint Anthony's, Father O'Malley was often slated for the confessionals. He heard many stories, from the tantrums in the supermarket when Mrs. Babcox tried to use an expired coupon to the Fishers filing for divorce, a third time, and always making their confessions together. Father O'Malley found his time spent in the booth inspiring, so much so that when the opportunity presented itself at the local paper he jumped at the chance. Now he writes for a syndicated gossip column.

THEIR WEDDINGS

The wedding was short and sweet. The bride and groom have been married before, about ten times between the two of them. They said they married for love; truth is they just love having a party. After the wedding ceremonies they had the best celebrations. They married each other the third and fifth time around and now they were at the altar for the tenth time. They were older; more experienced and had a lower tolerance for foolishness. They were perfect for each other. At sixty-four and seventy years old, they said they were finally ready to settle down.

DIRECT DEPOSIT

I shoulda paid more attention to bagging the groceries, but I couldn't help noticing what was happening in the parking lot of the A&P that October afternoon. As customers got to their cars to unload their groceries they stopped to pull money off their windshields. All I saw was a sea of green and white paper; turns out they were $100 bills on every car. The evening news reported a bank robbery took place down the street from the supermarket. There was a reward for any information related to the robbery. Months later no one has said a word.

DISCONNECTED

Anybody ever call you ugly before? Felicia Reynolds was called ugly nearly everyday of her young life, by her very own mother. Felicia was the youngest of seven children, by seven different daddies, and the only girl, but her mother didn't want her. Felicia's mother told her how she was trying for another boy and when Felicia was born, she was disappointed. On Felicia's tenth birthday her grandmother gave her a princess party, it was the best day of her life. That evening Felicia went to live with her grandmother, her mother lost custody of Felicia, due to negligence.

...AND FREEDOM FOR ALL

The truth was there, out in the open for everyone to see, but no one wanted to face it. Oh, they danced around it, not wanting to admit what they knew. They all thought they were not responsible; that they were *innocent*. Maybe they were to some degree, but instead of standing up for truth they turned their backs on it and left it behind. Over the years truth followed them. Sometimes it came as a dream or just a memory, but they could never escape it. For now, the truth waits patiently just to set them free.

KNOCK, KNOCK

The living always sees the dead before they pass away and for the past week Trevor had seen many of his dead relatives. It made him restless and he wouldn't dare fall asleep.

His last visitor was his mother, who died the year before, with a message: " Not now; come back later."
Trevor wanted to beat this disease and live longer.

Days later the doctor entered Trevor's hospital room, "Your blood work came back and your numbers look exceptionally good. It's a miracle!" Trevor sighed, "I've been playing games all my life, but I know now, life's no joke."

LIVING DOLLS

Felix Ugstad, is a famous shop owner living in Falkenberg, Sweden. As a boy, his father taught him how to make dolls. Felix studied engineering at the university and after he graduated, he continued to make dolls with greater enhancements than his father. His dolls were life-sized; they had smoother skin, different eye colors and defined bone structure, just to name a few features. Felix opened his unique store, Living Dolls, and when the opening was announced in town, people lined up for blocks. It seems, Felix designed the dolls so when they felt love they came to life.

REIGNING KING

I live like a king and I couldn't be happier. Not as a ruler of a nation or governing a people, but in my house, at thirty-six, I feel like I am a king. My basic needs are met daily and rarely am I lacking in any area. But it's not easy being in my position and having to make good judgment calls, because there are always demands being made on my life. My mother constantly asks me, "When are you going to move out of my house and get a place of your own?"

'TIL DEATH

The women at the Sunny Side retirement community were well aware of the charming Simeon Alexander; they called him Ex. Turns out he was married five times, to women with money, and was looking for wife number six. All five wives died suddenly, reportedly of natural causes. The women wondered if he had bad luck with women or whether he found ways to get rid of them. He wasn't single for long; by year's end he had a bride. Unfortunately, in the spring the women attended the funeral for Simeon Alexander, meanwhile his new wife left town with his fortune.

FAMILY JEWELS

Ramla, an African princess, loved being a mom. She raised eight children alone, seven boys and a girl, after her husband passed. She was determined that her precious jewels shined and made sure they were educated; got involved in cultural events; participated in community activities and spent time in worship as she showered them in love. Ramla's formula for success worked, for in her old age she was proud to have a professor, two doctors, a concert violinist, a business developer, an award winning novelist and two attorneys in the family. She knew her treasures would someday enrich the world.

THEN AGAIN

When I grow up I want to be an engineer, then again lawyers make a lot of money.

After college, I plan to work for the firm downtown, then again, that uptown company sounds better.

Marriage isn't for everyone, then again they say, "Third time's a charm!"

I'm planning for my retirement, this job is such a rat race, then again, I probably wouldn't keep still so I'd still work part time.

So now, I'm single again and my fourth wife said I was difficult to live with and indecisive. I think she's off base, then again, maybe she's right.

HOUSE WARMING

I've always wanted to be a parent. I have a bunch of nieces and nephews and my house has always been the party house for the family; I guess because I have the biggest backyard. Then when the celebrations are over everyone leaves and goes home and I'd be in the house alone. I never had a meaningful relationship; maybe I'm not lucky when it comes to love. I'm up there in age, but not a senior citizen yet. Recently, I started the paperwork for adoption and for the first time, I'll know how it feels to be a Dad.

BEGINNING TO END

Divorce. There I said it. I hate everything about it. My wife said it was over a year ago and asked for a trial separation; to me, that was for show. She was already set up with a new place and stopped having her mail come to the house. My ex-wife said she wasn't cut out to be anybody's wife; took her twelve years to figure it out though. It's time to start over and find a better definition of myself. I know there are plenty of opportunities waiting just for me. Beginning. There I said it. I'm ready.

WILL YOU WAIT FOR ME?

I don't have much to offer you now, but I'm working on it. No, I haven't been saying that for the past five years. Oh, you wrote down my five-year plan on paper? All right, maybe I didn't work hard enough on the last project and I missed out on that promotion, but you know I don't want to be at that job the rest of my life. I haven't stopped chasing my dream. No matter what, I want to live out that dream with you. So, don't make me ask too often, will you... just wait for me, okay?

LOOKING FOR LOVE

I'm thirty-three years old and I've only been in love once, ten years ago. I haven't trusted any other man with my heart since. I'm trying to find love, but is love lost? I know it's out there.... somewhere. I shouldn't let it bother me but when I see couples showing affection it makes me feel like I'm missing something in life. I've been meaning to help out at the animal rescue shelter; I have lots of love to spread around and they need love too. Who knows, maybe love might find me giving and bring some lovin' my way.

BONDING IN MATRIMONY

When asked their advice on how they've managed to stay married for over fifty years, the adoring couple said:

Husband: "Being married takes hard work, but I treat it like a business. Sometimes you have to get up early to get things running and stay up late to take stock of inventory."

Wife: "I agree with my husband, but he left out one of the key ingredients. You gotta make sure you make the customer happy, because they'll always come looking for what you have to offer."

Husband: "Thanks, dear. That's the kind of support you'll need to keep going."

WE'RE FAMILY

My parents are robots, don't misunderstand me, they don't act like robots, they're actually robots, but I'm human. Our second parents took my two younger sisters and me in after the terrible war in 2045. We were trying to live on our own after we got separated from our first parents. Robin and Robert wanted to provide a safe and loving home for three young girls who needed a family. We've gotten our share of stares and snickers from a few people who don't get how we're a real family. It's simple; family is defined by the love you share.

HANDLING REJECTION

You've been ignoring me for so long, I should be used to it, but I know I can't give up. My heart keeps telling me to go on despite your actions toward me. You don't seem to mind the gifts that I've given you; you take them with great pleasure, as you say, "I deserve it." You won't entertain any conversation longer than a few minutes because you claim I don't understand you and what's happening in your life. But son, parents know a lot more than you think they do, that's why they don't give up on their children.

LIVE BY EXAMPLE

I want to be just like my mother; she's successful, a leader and she knows how to get what she wants, even my dad stands clear of her when she's on a mission. Mom is an agent for the Special Services Alliance, where she travels and provides hope for refugees. She told me when she started her job she didn't want to leave her family to go on assignments. I told her the time she spent away only made the time we were together more special. Mom is my hero because of her unselfish nature and strength as a woman.

MAKING MISTAKES

Growing up in an Asian household was challenging because there was an expectation to be perfect. In school, sports and even music, my parents wanted my sister and me to excel more than others. They were always bragging about their perfect daughters. When I got older, I moved to London, to escape the pressure of my parents; I met a fine young architect there. We got married a year ago and now we're expecting a baby. I never knew there was so much to prepare for. I don't want to make a mistake; I just want everything to be perfect.

HOLDING ON TO MEMORIES

After years of driving a truck, Walton planned out how he would spend his time when he was done. Traveling from coast to coast of the U.S., he's been many places and seen nearly everything; the only thing he missed, was seeing his four sons grow into men. They had their own families now, living in different parts of the world. Walton bought four airline tickets hoping to visit his sons; they all agreed to see him. He couldn't go back and be a better father, but he could spend time with them and let things just be.

WHOSE LIFE IS IT ANYWAY?

I've always wanted to work in finance, travel the world and make a name for myself. My dad convinced me to become a dentist, just like him; we work for the same practice. A few years later, mom suggested I settle down and start a family. After dating for seven years, I finally married my longtime girlfriend and we moved out to the suburbs. My wife thought we should have a baby, now my son will carry on the family name. Funny, I thought my life would have turned out a lot differently.

GET UP AND GO

I grew up in a military family and we've lived in many places. My older brother and I thought of it as an adventure every time we moved. I enjoy traveling and now that I'm an adult, I travel extensively as a jewelry designer. Having the freedom to fly out from my hometown to any destination of my choosing is exhilarating. My friends think I'm strange because I always carry my passport and have a "GO" bag in the car. The bag is packed with everything I need for a trip so when the moment strikes, I'm ready to go.

CENTER STAGE

Ladies and Gentlemen, thank you for attending the performance today. As you may know the production has been in development for many years now, to make it the best it's ever been. **It's About Me,** is a dynamic one-woman show that was written, produced and directed by moi. The show has drama, mystery and some comedic moments. I'm sure everyone will enjoy it as much as I have enjoyed the rehearsals. Sorry, there are no refunds, but once you see the performance you'll probably tell your friends all about me. Okay, let's go ahead and start the show.

MARCHING FORWARD

Mississippi, in 1962, Sam, a white boy and Bernie, a black boy had been the best of friends since they were little, but now some folks thought they shouldn't be. They grew up in the same neighborhood and did most things together, even throughout their college years. Bernie and Sam participated in marches; sit-ins and even got arrested and went to jail together. This was during the civil rights movement, when tempers were high and tolerance was scarce. Through the years, they've remained close and stayed in touch. They grew to become brothers and never let hatred tear them apart.

WALKING AWAY

She's packing up her bags again. She's really not going through with this, is she? She's responsible for everything here...she holds it all together... she can't walk away from that. Okay, it's not easy living with Dad; he's as tough as nails and acts like a drill sergeant, but that's only sometimes. Yeah, she's left before, but that wasn't for long; she came back about a week later and things went back to normal. I know she still loves me, doesn't she? I still have a lot to learn from her, I'm only twelve. Moooooooom, come back!

LOSING WEIGHT

Ah...it feels good to get rid of my extra weight, the best feeling I've had in years. I can do a lot more with my life since I don't have all that weight. How did I do it? Well, let me tell you, it wasn't easy but after I made the decision, I worked hard and stuck with my commitment. After living with the extra weight for so long, I didn't think I could ever get rid of my two-timing, low-down, no-good cheating ex-husband. Thank God he's no longer in my life. Two hundred pounds, gone (snap) like that.

MOUNTAIN TOP EXPERIENCE

At the peak of Japan's Rangoon Mountain a sweet young couple, Tadashi and Setsu, made a small cottage their home. Each morning they'd climb to the top of the mountain to enjoy it's beauty. Setsu gathered flowers to bring back home while Tadashi would close his eyes to touch the clouds. They weren't in need of anything; they had what they wanted. Their living was simple; they would give thanks, take care of the land and share their love. They've lived alone in the mountains for many years, fulfilling their mission to be closer to God.

WHO'S JUDGING?

One drink can't do any harm. It's so smooth, as it cascades down the back of my throat. One glass, to help calm my nerves. Mmm, comforting, just like a good woman. A little something to take the edge off. I mean a couple of drinks won't let me lose focus; I can still sit up straight. It's not like it's everyday, only in the afternoons and maybe a few beers on the weekends. Stress comes with the job, so I gotta find balance. Court is back in session…let me make my way back on the bench.

FOR THE LOVE OF FRIENDSHIP

Friendships are fantastic things to have. Finding someone who you can share things in common with and have fun with can sometimes be challenging. You're fortunate when you have a buddy, a pal, who'll follow you to places others wouldn't dare. The friendship allows you freedom to be yourself whether you're just fooling around or being fancy. You don't fret or freak out when you stumble upon the seriousness of life because you have faith that somebody's got your back. For all you do for others, it's fabulous to know that a true friend will do the same for you.

IN THE CLOUD

Super heroes are just ordinary people with extraordinary talents. We are the ones you call in a crisis, to lend a hand when no one else is around. For decades, the public has put their confidence in our reliability, which we all appreciate, and the thank yous and applause are great, but they fade fast. When we take off our costumes and masks, underneath we're just like anyone else. We do get lonely. Everyone could use a hero; just remember heroes could **use** someone too.

COMING HOME

Buster, our golden retriever, has been part of the family since she was a pup. Our youngest named her and said she looked like she could take care of herself. Buster was always first at the dinner table and always found her way snuggled in my favorite chair, before I scooted her off. While raking leaves in the yard, last fall, Buster took off running through the gate, down the street and into the back of a waiting pickup truck. A year later, my favorite chair is still empty, just waiting, hoping, that someday Buster will come back home.

PASSING MOMENTS

I sat down on a park bench today, for the first time in years, only because I took the time to clear my busy schedule. Six months ago, according to the police report, the driver ran the light, rushing to get to an appointment...he, only had minor scratches but I lost my husband in the car crash. On the bench I thought about how hectic life had become...time was passing by, but life has a way of reminding us to slow down and enjoy the moments. That's something I'll pass on to my baby, when I give birth next month.

SOOTHING MUSIC

My Dad has this thing he does when I'm sad, he plays me upbeat tunes on his ukulele. He's been doing it since Mom passed away. Dad found me sitting in the back of my closet crying my eyes out. He leaned over and gave me a hug, then without saying a word he left the room and came back with his ukulele. I'm almost eighteen now, soon I'll go away to college and I know I'll miss my Dad. I'm not sad, but I want to hear my Dad play, so I let him think I am sometimes.

RAISED UP RIGHT

"He's slow," they said "he'll never get it like the other kids." That's what Sebastian's teachers told his dad and I when he was eight years old. They looked at him but not his potential. You see, Sebastian has dyslexia, so what he would see was in reverse. We nurtured his mind and strengthened his abilities with practical learning tools that would become second nature to him. Sebastian excelled in academics and community activities. He was the valedictorian at his college graduation and in his speech he said, "Thanks to my parents for helping me to turn my life around."

NEIGHBORHOOD WATCH

My neighbor is such a busybody; she's into nearly everything that happens in the neighborhood. Like when there was that car accident, she was right there on the corner giving an eyewitness account. She even notices the misbehaving children and knows which house to report them to. Her curiosity proved useful the day a stranger broke into our house, across the street from her house. By the time the thief made it out the front door, the cops had already pulled up and caught him red-handed. Our family is grateful to her for keeping an eye on things around here.

LOVE CHAT

Listen, Love, we need to talk. I don't get what you're doing to me. Sometimes you make me feel like I'm on top of the world, and at other times, I want to shut everyone out. We tried to get together years ago, but the timing wasn't right. Now, you got me doing things I ordinarily wouldn't do and it makes me a little nervous, but I'm willing. We need to figure out how to get along. It may seem strange, me talking to my heart, but you know it's worth it for my girl; she means everything to me.

PULLING PUNCHES

Round 1 The opponent came out swinging with rage and anger.

Round 2 The opponent quenched his thirst then stared down his challenger, trying to intimidate her.

Round 3 The bell rang, the opponent struck again. He swung and missed as she bobbed and weaved.

Round 4 Before he could ready his fist to strike again, she stood her ground and fought back. She was declared the champion, then she walked away.

Round 5 The opponent stood alone in the middle of the ring wondering how he lost the fight. He underestimated his challenger, not realizing the strength within her.

DESTINED

Carter and Alli lived in the same neighborhood for sixteen years. In high school their homeroom classes were two doors away from each other. They took the express train to work every morning from the Dunbar station. Alli was an accountant and Carter was an analyst for the same firm and they had never met until one year at the company Christmas party. They got married and enjoyed forty-two years of wedded bliss. Alli took ill and passed away after a long battle. Six months later, Carter passed on as well. Now their love will last throughout time.

LET'S NOT PRETEND

You and me haven't been we for a long time now. I don't know. Have you noticed how far we've drifted apart? I want things to work, but I just don't know how. I want to be strong, but it's so hard to hold on. I think back when we were friends you showed me how much you cared. We spent time getting to know each other and then we fell in love. Today, we're not the same, I don't know who we've become. Let's not pretend anymore, it's time for us to begin again, maybe with other people.

TRAILING BEHIND

We may live in a trailer, but heaven help us, we ain't trash. I made this place home for Bobby Ray and the kids for the past eight years. It's been hard saving up for a house because Bobby Ray's work ain't steady, but we can't give up. We do the best we can with what we got and live a clean life. God knows it ain't easy some days, trying to catch up to the same kinda living like most folk. We don't beg, borrow or steal, we just try to stretch a dollar as far it can go.

UNFORGETTABLE

For the past few years I've led some to believe that I'm steadily losing my memory. It was at my 86th birthday party when I broke my leg after a fall from dancing. While recovering my kids came to visit and had a chat while they thought I was asleep. They talked about power of attorney and liquidating my assets and as I opened my eyes the conversation changed. That day I developed a plan to protect my future and to forget my three ungrateful children. Without my wife, there just wasn't a family anymore, only memories to hold onto.

CYCLE OF LIFE

I had four children, two sons, two daughters and my wife, then there was a car accident.

I had three children, one son, two daughters and my wife. My baby girl drowned in the neighbor's pool.

I had two kids, a son, a daughter and my wife.   Leukemia was the diagnosis and took our boy.

I still had a daughter and my wife, but then it was bittersweet when we welcomed the twins, unfortunately I lost my wife during childbirth.

Today, I have two daughters, a son and a greater appreciation for how precious life is.

ROCKY TIMES

How do you start over again? My family and I moved to Tulsa from Detroit when a lot of the factories closed down and we lost our jobs. After six months our new house was broken into twice, and our van broke down and needed repair. My wife said, "we gotta keep praying for change," I was reluctant, but I prayed anyway. An insurance agent called us weeks later to let us know we had a sizeable check waiting for us. Sometimes when you slip down into the valley, you still have the rocks to climb back up the mountain.

FIRE DRILL

Running. Heavy breathing. What a workout. Fire trucks pass by. Police sirens blaring behind me. I see a house on fire. Wait a minute; I can't believe it. That's my house in flames, Lord, help me! Why us, how could this horrible thing have happened? I push through the crowd to get a little closer. There is so much commotion; people yelling; glass breaking. My entire family was home when I left. Where are they now, Rachel, Billy, Jessica? Oh my God, are they inside? Tears flow down my face. The fire gets worse. I feel hopeless. What's that? "Daddy!"

TRUST ME

My man, He is something else and He knows how to take care of me. We've been together over a decade now, after meeting at church. I heard about Him from some friends, they were bragging about how good He was and all the kind things He'd done for them, so I decided to check Him out for myself. Let me tell you, He didn't disappoint. After all these years though...I still don't trust Him like I should. Yet, without fail, He comes through for me every time because He's a man of His word. God, I love Him.

ABOUT THE AUTHOR

Mercedes Douglas has been writing for many years beginning with her love of poetry and short stories. While in college she discovered her untapped talent for writing children's stories. Mercedes continues to work on several projects, which include children's books, YA novel and an adult novel. She enjoys all things crafty, gardening and traveling. She lives near Atlanta, GA with her husband, Stefan and their dog, Sophia.

You can find Mercedes on social networking sites where she's always excited to share information and meet people. Connect with her at the following sites:

Facebook: www.facebook.com/mercedesdouglas
Twitter: @mercedesdwriter
Email: md@mercedesdouglas.com